The Eternal Bartender Replies
David Macpherson

Note from the Writer

I don't have much memory writing this. On editing it today, I was reminded of some of it, but most of it is kind of a mystery.

I wrote these interconnected stories in 2017, seven years ago. Why did I not put them out back then? I really don't know. The stories are nothing to be ashamed of. Also, one of the stories was published in a slightly different form in a volume of the Black Scat Review. I do not know which story or what issue of the review. But the bulk of this work remained on a harddrive for nearly a decade.

I used to drink a lot when I wrote this. I don't drink anymore. I don't know if there is a connection between that and it not getting published until now.

I am writing this to say I don't write like this anymore. One would hope that if I have not improved my writing in seven years, I probably have at least changed some of the style.

I am of the odd belief that if I wrote it, I should publish it. You might read this book and think, "There are times when publishing is not prudent." But who knows, you might dig it. I never know what people will like to read. Might as well give you everything I got and leave it to you decide whether that was the right place of action or not.

No matter what, enjoy.

David

June 28, 2024

The Eternal Bartender on the Act of Lying at Taverns

Bar Truth: Everyone drinking at a bar is lying to one degree or another.

Pat, the eternal bartender, replies: How true that is. You know what they say about lawyers, how you can tell they're lying. The answer being, their mouths are moving. With bar goers, they don't have to even open their yap holes to be liars. As soon as that drink is in front of them, there is lying going on. The lies range from "I can handle this next drink" to "Man, I am a handsome devil and that chick would be lucky to know me." Sometimes I think we charge less for the booze and more for the mendacity.

Now, there are lies and there are lies. I have seen my share of insane storytellers who actually think they're on the up and up. The biggest liar? That's hard to say, but I remember one fella way back when I was working behind the stick at this wine bar round Gallelli or them parts. Man, those were sandal and tunic times, not the best for sartorial pleasure, but that's what we was wearing then, so what you going to do?

There was this fella, he had a following. Back then, you talk fine and weighty, you had people listening at you like you was better than the rest. This guy was alright, polite, tipped, didn't give me no guff most of the time. But the stories he told. He sure went on. It wasn't that he was smarter or prettier in his tales, but that he could do things. He said he cured the handicapped. He made blind people see, the lame walk, the lepers have Oil of Olay type skin and no doubt, he made the stinky take baths. Now that's a miracle.

When this fella was really in his cups, said he was the son of God. Now that's a DNA test I would like to see run.

The last time he was in my joint, he was telling a tale about his latest daring do. He had word that a buddy of his was sick and dying. Instead of going to see him right away, the fella dawdled, probably tossing back a few in my establishment, I wouldn't be surprised. He finally got around to seeing this friend of his and the dude was dead four days. The fella said he went to his buddy's tomb and commanded him to rise and come out. Then what did that dead dude do? He rose and came out. Madness.

All of the fella's followers were open mouthed and excited by this bullshit. I had enough of it and told him and his toadies to hit the road, I was cutting them off. No one talks resurrection in my joint.

The fella never raised his voice, he was polite like I said. He told me he wasn't done imbibing. I told him not here he ain't. He said that was cool and could he have a jug of water. I asked why. He said he was going to go out to a field and turn it into wine. I threw up my hands. I gave the water to him and told him to have at it. He left with all his thirsty followers behind him.

Never saw him again. I guess he found another joint to tell his stories. There is always some place to tell them, and some sucker to listen to them like they're true.

The Eternal Bartender on the Horror of Bar Food

Bar Truth: Sometimes food served at a bar is more trouble than it's worth.

Pat, the eternal bartender, responds: The one thing wrong with that statement is the word sometimes. Bar food is always more trouble than any fella working behind the stick should ever wrestle with. Now you don't have to tell me that in the beginning of times bars were taverns that served a meal with the ale you was quaffing. I was there, I know. But establishments can evolve over time and we now have the perfect product, the bar. The saloon. The local joint. The place where you get pie eyed on drink and that's it. It is a finely honed creation, it took some time to get there, but it is sleek and resilient, able to survive a nuclear attack, like the cockroach.

For some reason, there's always someone trying to get you to think that you need food with this. This is crazy talk. You can tell it's crazy talk from the food they try to foist on us barkeeps to peddle. Pickled eggs. Drunken pineapple slices. Jerky. I'll say it again, jerky. That's not a food name, that's a way to describe the kind of person who orders this rubbish. You got your peanuts, and your pretzels and now you have your buffalo wings and jalapeno poppers. This ain't proper. This is a fried slap in the face of every good publican.

All of these things just ruin the flavor of the booze you're drinking. Food is a heathen thing in a joint. I know, hell I helped create one of the biggest bar foods around. Pretty ashamed of it, but I ain't holding nothing back, I can admit mistakes.

I was working the bar at this hoity toity club for annoying lords in Jolly Old Blimey, mixing a lot of sweet wine cocktails and totties, nonsense drinks but that's what the tipping customers were after. In the back room of the joint was a table for cards. These Lords, Dukes and

Earls were crazy for gambling. Bad at it too. There was this one Earl who was blowing threw his granddaddy's money like it was a six pack of Schlitz through a body. This guy was the terrible combination of not being good at cards and not being smart enough to know it.

He was an angry fella when he lost, which is my way of saying he was angry all the time. I remember it was getting to dawn and my deal was I couldn't close shop until all the gentlemen were done with their "entertainments." He was losing money and no one wanted to stop playing because he was just giving the store away to them. I had enough and went to him and said, "M'lord." Christ, the crap I had to say to keep me in beer and graces. "M'lord, it is quite late and you have not had anything to eat. You should end the evening and repair to your house for breakfast."

I had to repeat that a few times before the idiot Earl heard me. Finally he allowed himself to look at me and said, "My man, I have a fine hand here and I cannot allow myself to stop. True, I am famished, so just go and find me something I can eat with one hand, for I must not cease."

These landed gentry were always a pain in the ass. So I went to the butler's pantry and looked at what was there. All I found was a stale two day old loaf of bread and last week's mutton. I thought, this will teach him. I will make a lousy meal for a lousy tipper. I cut the bread in two and sliced up the tough, nasty meat. I put the meat in between the bread, pressed down hard and served it to the Earl on a chipped plate.

He ate it in one hand, like he said. He chewed that stale bread, that tough meat for days it seems. But he loved it, because he won. He finally had a good streak, and he credited it to the meal I gave him. He played until noon, I was exhausted.

Then every time he came he asked for that thing with meat between bread, said it was good luck. Then other loser gamblers started asking for it, by this lousy Earl's name. Sandwich.

And that my friends, is why we suffer to this day eating lousy sandwiches. Not because they're good, but because it allows you to keep on drinking and losing money.

I try not to work at places that sell food. Sometimes I do, but never if they have sandwiches on the menu. Even if they hide it by calling it a panini or a sub or what not. I know better. Not for me. Let me pour drinks and be happy, for once.

The Eternal Bartender and the Creative Essence of Drinking Establishments

Bar Truth: Great Ideas are found in bars, but are not always understood the next day.

Pat, the Eternal Bartender, replies: Yeah, that's the way it is with a lot of things at the old bar. I mean jokes which are the funniest things in the world on the third round, get blank stares and you-hadda-be-theres the next morning. But that doesn't mean the joke wasn't funny. It was, its just that the sober world is not ready for it. And its more than just jokes, great ideas that people come up with at bars have changed the very world. I ain't kidding.

I was working a beer and schnitzel joint that was popular with young physisicts, apprentice pastry chefs and grave diggers, way back in 1904 or so and this patent clerk was coming in for the cheap beers. He was a weird guy with great crazy hair. Al. That was him, wasn't it? Well one day he came in more disoriented than usual and he shoved a bar napkin right at me. It had some writing on it. He said, "I wrote this, but I do not know what it means. I wrote it here last night and I don't know what it means."

I looked at the paper and read it out, "Ee equals emm see two."

Al pulled at his hair and said, "No E equals MC squared. I wrote it but those pilsners wiped me clear. I can't recall what it means at all, but look at it. That is the prettiest equation I have ever seen. I don't know what it means, but I want it to mean something. I want it to be more than just a looker of an equation."

These young physicists were always like this, they made no sense and they tipped in weird derivations of binomial theories so I wasn't keen to be helpful. But I'm a bartender and I can't not do something, it's in our blood. That and whisky.

So I looked at who was there at the stools and there was a lot of these wannabe scientists, it was an odd joint and I gathered them all together and told them the problem. "Al here has a sweet equation without a concept. Can you boys help a kid out?" To make it worth their while, I opened up the tap on the Special, a pretty good double bock we had a surplus on. There was a cheer and all the scientists, apprentice pastry chefs and grave diggers went at it.

They shouted out what e was and they figured it was energy and m was mass. I don't know who thought the mass was the mass of all things but it had to be a pastry chef because they measure everything precisely even though all they have to do is put sugar in and things even out. More weirdness happened of course, but that's what happens when the special double bock is flowing. Whoever came up with the idea that c being the speed of light had to be one of the drunker grave diggers because that idea was a crazy deep but not deep enough kind of concept.

Al was bewildered, but was nodding going "Ja, ja, I don't understand this, but I can swing it out and make it work"

And I guess he did. Now I ain't sure but I think the nature of the universe worked differently before that night. But then those drunks came up with a definition for a few letters and numbers and the nature of the universe altered itself so that it would actually make sense. That's the power of a good bar, it can make the universe conform to a good story.

The next year I heard Al found a way to bullshit the details and publish his Special Theory of Relativity. The reason it's called the special theory, because they were drinking the Special I had on tap. The universe is still recovering from the hangover of that night. I don't think it ever will.

The Eternal Bartender and the Besmirching of Bar Napkins

Bar Truth: Though money is the preferred form of transaction for drinks, artwork has been an option for artists who are not in the chips

Pat, the Eternal Bartender, replies: Yeah, but I wish that wasn't the case. There are too many guys who think themselves Picasso and want to give me their prints or photos instead of paying for their beer and pretzels. This is all I say no to. They get right pissed, but I can be pretty granite. A lot more solid than the art they try to pawn off on me. I mean, really. Most of this is awful. I rather you pay for your pilsner than give me a crappy painting of a balloon dog. Yeah, I got offered that, and the guy not only offered me the painting, but wanted me to sign a disclaimer that I would not try to reproduce the work or resell it. I pushed the painting and this contract back at him shook him until enough coins came out of his clothes to pay for the Budweiser, with a little extra for me. Got to look out for my bottom line in this crazy art world.

And now there are artists who don't use paint or anything that might seem like art to me. There's those performance based conceptual artist. How can I accept a performance piece as payment? I don't want some fella stripping down to nothing and standing on one foot as a statement against, I don't know, clothes and feet I suppose. How many shots of whiskey is that worth? To me, I have a number in mind. It's zero.

Every week I have to turn down someone's art. And every time I said to these cheapskates, no can't do it, you ain't no Picasso.

I know this because I knew Picasso. Even he was no Picasso, most of the time.

I was working a cafe joint in Gay Paree, looking fine in a starched white apron and slicked back hair. I was a regular swell with the wines and aperitifs. One of the regulars was the artist, Pablo. Pay in the ass. He was so famous at this point he didn't bring a wallet. He was too big for that. He was world famous, women loved his wrinkly butt, and he kind of smelled. Not of success, but of old cabbage.

Now I ain't got nothing against my clientele smelling of any food products, it allows me to identify them quickly, without turning around to see them. But I got something against an old man who smells of old cabbage and doesn't pay his tab. You could smell of morning dew and whiskey scented candy canes and if you don't pay on time, I will think that you stink.

Pablo was so famous, he just doodled on a napkin and said that this was an original Picasso and worth so much more than the wine he downed.

The lousy part was, my boss told me to accept these doodles for payment. Can you believe it? It is a complete breakdown of the bartender-customer accord. That highly vaunted relationship says: you drink, you pay.

It wouldn't have been so bad if the doodles were any good. They were clowns, and cats, and sort of women, but ugly ones that got their faces too close to an industrial hand mixer. But the boss was happy. He was selling them for a hundred francs a piece to tourists.

That was the real problem. We were having more and more tourists come for these ugly drawings. They were clamoring for them. No accounting for taste. But the boss wanted to sell as many as possible, he was getting 100 francs a pop for doodles on a bar napkin. We ran out of our stock of Picasso IOUs, excuse me, his well executed works of art. Yeah, hard to say that with a straight face.

We tried to get Picasso to drink more, owing us more drawings. But that Pablo was a mean cuss and got annoyed with us and moved his custom to another cafe. The louse.

"Pat, you gots to do something about this," the owner says to me. What was I supposed to do? We had no more doodles. So I took it into my own hands. Literally. With a pencil. I saw enough of those terrible Picasso drawings, I knew I could do better.

Over one night, and three bottles of cheap whisky, I made a sheaf of new Picasso napkin drawings. Pretty spiffy. We sold them. Some of the customers complained as they handed over their hundred francs. "My kid could draw something like that." Well, maybe your kid draws shit like that, but could he draw a perfect draft of stout, like me? I highly doubt that.

I moved on to another bar, like I do. Picasso saw me one day and said he figured I was ruining his name with my forgeries. "Why Pablo," I asked, "you have had forgers before. Not as handsome as me, but that's a given. So why are you so bothered, my stuff can't be any worse than the slap dash shit you made yourself."

"That's the problem," Picasso said. "They weren't worse than mine. They were better. I don't want the art I make to pay off my bar tabs to be any good. I want it to be awful. I want the fine work to be on the canvas. I want the work that's closest to money, paying for my wine, to be awful. My people expect it that way, and your acceptable scribbles are ruining my reputation."

"Well, that's just stupid," I said. And I tossed the freeloader out.

Yeah, art used for paying for your drink? I'm against it. Now, if what you gave me was an original black velvet image of dogs playing poker, well, the drinks are on me.

The Eternal Bartender and the Twirling Rum Bottle of Death

Bar Truth: With the popularity of flair bartending, the bartender is an actual entertainer.

Pat, the eternal bartender, replies: I hate flair bartending. It is the skin cancer on the body of salooning. The idea that people pack into a bar to watch stupid stick monkees flip a bottle in the air and then pour drinks. Behind the head. Through the legs. Heading right for my head, splitting it in two. My head is split in two because of flair bartending.

I am not an entertainer. I am a pourer of beer. I will shake a cocktail with vigor, put a good deal of elbow into it, but I am not tossing an unsuspecting bottle of vodka up towards the ceiling, ass over teakettle. I have too much respect for the bottle of booze to do that to them. I mean, there they are, a passing bottle of rum. All it wants to do is be lightly bent over and it will give up its liquor. You toss it twirling up into the air. It gets sick to its stomach. Booze bottles are gentle creatures and don't deserve such handling. And if the rum bottle is sick to it's stomach, just think how lousy the booze is when it finally reaches your glass.

More than that, I have too much respect for the bottom line of any joint I'm working to flair out. When one of those idiots spins a bottle, there is always some liquor escapes in the twisting. That might splash the customers, or worse, it might hit me, the bartender minding his own business, just making drinks next to the idiot booze juggler. Even if it misses the clientele, booze will hit the floor. That's booze that will never see the bottom of a high ball glass, it will never graduate to mixed drink status, or settle down and get into a relationship with a few dashes of bitters. That's a sad lonely shot of nothing.

That's just booze puddling on the floor. Making the bar area sticky and losing the owner of the place some dough. You might not think it's a lot, only a little escapes when you toss the bottle, but multiply it by all the times that bottle is upended and that can rob the till something considerable.

There is a lot of skill and practice that these yahoos have to work on, for what? For honoring the patrons with an even longer wait time for their drink? That's going to get a tip. That's going to get a knife thrown at you.

Actually, I remember a few bartenders who could deflect a tossed knife with their twirling bottles. Course I did, cause flair bartending used to be a martial art.

As a keeper of the peace, as all good bartenders are, I don't go for any karate kung fu nonsense when things get wiley at the joint. I like the classics: a sawed off pool cue, an ax handle or any old hammer. Why get fancy? There is nothing special about a drunken bar fight, so the way to suppress should be as simple. But I saw Flair Fu once it worked. Not it wasn't called that, but give me a break, I'm calling it something here, alright?

I was working a tent out by a work site, when they were building the railroad. They had a lot of rowdiness and the whiskey was foul. There were hourly bar fights and blood was used as an accent color in all decorative flourishes. This is what bartending should always be about.

The proprietor was a cowhand and he tried to lasso and hogtie the more prominent of the scrappers. But lasso does not work in a bar, even if it's a tent and most of the drinking happens in the fresh air. There is just not enough room to get the rope around the knuckler and it was impossible to get over to them when subdued to tie em up. It was a mess. A great mess.

The dishwasher we hired on was from China. Originally, he worked the rails, setting down tracks. A pick ax took his left eye, so he washed dishes. He could still work the rails, but he thought providence was advising him to find another vocation. One day, he was spit cleaning the glassware, as was the fashion when a fight broke out. Two big guys bumped into each other and kept on bumping. Normally, this would do nothing to make us look up, but one of the big galoots had a knife and tossed it. It was coming right at me.

Now no one needs to worry about me. I eat the knives thrown in a bar fight for breakfast. I actually can stare down an incoming knife and make it whimper and scurry back home to knife drawer. But I wasn't looking right at it. The dishwasher was.

He did a leap forward and cartwheeled over to me and then passed toward the shelf that held our bottles. He took two bottles of shine and spun them behind his head. One of them made it to his right hand and pulled forward and the spinning bottle hit the knife. WIth the bottle twirling like it did, the force brought the knife to the ground. But while I watched this, the second bottle rocketed straight into the head of the bar brawler. That guy's legs kicked out and he fell hard to the ground.

That wasn't the end of it, because then the other drunks watching were ticked that the guy got knocked out by a Chinese fella. Drunks and their pride, both make you do and say tactically questionable things and both get pissed out into a pot the next morning. They all went after my dishwasher.

I tried to stop them, but it was a wave that went right past me. But I didn't have to worry too much. There were still bottles on the shelf. He took two more and did twists and turns. He did slow turns on the bottle which caused the liquor to splash out. But not willy nilly. All of the liqour shot into the eyes of the incoming yahoos. Now I don't need to tell you, there was no such thing as a top shelf for this bar. All the booze was the bottom of the well.

They liquor stung and blinded these guys but good. But that wasn't all. The dishwasher took two more bottles, tossed them end over end high into the air. While they were spinning like gyroscopes, he forward flipped toward the brawlers. He landed on his feet, held out his hands and a bottle landed in each of his hands. He then clubbed the guys where were still clawing at their eyes.

Now some of my customers weren't too happy that a Chinese took out their pardners and started in on the dishwasher. That guy smiled and started tossing the bottles in close fast circles. So fast it was hard to actually see the damned rot gut. You could feel it, it was making wind like a monsoon. Blew two of the fellas right over. Any that got close to him, he clubbed down.

It was a bad moment for the fighters when one took out a knife or a pick. That's when the dishwasher went super fast. He tossed a bottle at one guy taking out a sticker. The bottle hit hard on the head and then twirled right back into dishwasher's hand. There was a spray of whiskey that shot out from the bottle. The entire stream landed in a glass on the bar. I picked up the glass and taste tested the bouquet. It seemed fine to me.

These things take forever in memory, but this whole scuffle lasted no more than a minute. My fellow bar worker flattened an entire train camp of idiots in a few seconds. I gave him a long slow clap of approval.

He was breathing a little harder than usual, but not much. I said, "Something alright. Now can you do that while mixing drinks? People would love to see that and get a fine glass at the end. I can see a franchise for such a thing. Twirling drinks could charge more."

Yes, I know. I'm being honest, but that was really me, promoting flair. I was young then and the rush of the fight must have played with my thinking. Thank god the dishwasher wasn't having that nonsense anywhere near him.

He said, "This is an ancient art. A martial art. Finer than the forms that use only hand and foot. The liquor bottle is the purest form of defense. My people would never allow such a skill, such a holy calling to be used for mixing drinks. How could I ever face my family when next I see them if I did such a base thing?"

Boy was he right. Sad to admit, I never learned his name. The boss fired him that night for starting a fracas. Like I said, no good comes from flair bartending.

The Eternal Bartender Reads the Numbers on His Customers

Bar Truth: Bartenders can tell the fate of their clientele just by looking at their face

Pat, the Eternal Bartender, responds: That depends, but mostly that's true. I mean I look at a thirsty fella with his money palmed in his hand and I know his future. This guy's going to get a little anesthetic and I will be a tad richer. The twitchy guy who comes in and barks his order to me and sneers at his stool mate, I can foresee the attempted fight he will perpetrate and the sawed off cue stick that will work the side of his head. Who needs tea leaves? I have the second sight. Actually, I run bars, I don't like tea leaves being anywhere near me and my amazing fortune telling abilities.

But I think what you are asking about this, the numerology of hard drinking. We keepers of the faith and the booze can always read these numbers, portents. There is the one people always talk about, the elevenses. That's when a right drunk comes in and the two cords on the back of his neck are sticking out. All the rest of his flesh has fallen away, gone with their faulty liver and sense of hope. You know, the things you don't need. But the elevenses, they pop up, looking like a number eleven. We bartenders see that and whistle low.

That's the sign of death coming. This guy is done. We are talking weeks, not months. We are talking about shot glasses of life left, not fifth of a gallon bottles of it. We don't tell the guy what's going to happen. That's not our responsibility. We just notice it and give him a little extra on the pours. What's it to the bar if we give a little extra push to the final last call, it's doing everyone a favor.

But that's easy stuff for even a newbie bartender to pick up. There are other numbers that show up on a fella. With a good eye and enough experience, you can read all the numbers that ride up on a body.

Now a guy coming in might have dark rings around his eyes with a black tail coming off the left side of the circle. What's around his eyes, that is what we call the lazy sixes and that means he's drinking to forget a woman. As the weeks go on, you can see the tail fade and then the circles fade. The drinking doesn't stop, but at least he don't look like a lovestruck raccoon.

Now I haven't seen it in centuries, but men grabbed at their mugs of beer and in the space between the thumb and fingers were two black circles touching each other. That's the eights. That tells us that what we got is a serious down on his luck drinker who stopped for a while. They got on the wagon. They were too broke to belly up to the bar. They had a nagging influence stopping him from doing the good works of a fine drunk. It don't matter, all that matters is that he was a lush and he stopped for some time. But now he was returned to the fold and this beer is the first on his way back. You can see the eights as he grabbed the mug and takes it to his lips. When he puts the cup down with a happy clatter, the mark is gone. A good riddance too.

If a fella comes in with an eighty six written on his forehead with a black sharpie it means that he is never going to get into that fraternity he was rushing. It's up to us fine purveyors of booze to take his mind off the fact that it will be weeks before those numbers wash off. Permanent markers are the work of the devil, I always say.

I have seen crop circle like collections of pimples on a man's head that are usually a circle with a few pimples dead in the center. We call it the big zero. It means that the guy got away with a crime. Not a mamby pamby run of the mill crime like shoplifting or extortion or high risk jaywalking. Nah, the big zero only shows up with bank robbers, highway men and murderers. This is not the kind of customer you want. Little known fact, but cold blooded killers top badly. And these are the kind of guys you can't complain to. I might talk back to a pickpocket about the lightness of the tip. But someone with blood on the hands, you thank them and move on. I see a guy come in with a big zero, I know the loser for the evening is me and my diminished take home pay.

A guy coming in with a 215 made up from stray graying whiskers on his chin is a talker. The whiskers grow that way from all the jawing they doing. Even their chin hairs get annoyed at all the speechifying and have turned white. Now a bar likes conversation. But blowhards is something that has nothing to do with a good one. I see that shaggy tuft of numbers and throw them right out. I mean the only blowhard jawer allowed in a joint I run is me. Thank you very much.

I only saw this once, but other people working behind the stick have attested to it, but the seven birthmark is one people don't mind coming across. It's a big number. The top goes across the entire forehead in deep purple and then it crosses down the length of the face. It's not a pretty sight. Usually, the numerology we come across is something only the bartender knows about, but the seven folks know about. The seven on the face says that this guy makes a fine one night stand. Will not be pushy and leave when asked. I have had a few women say they are always hoping to find one of those. Not because they were desperate women, they were good people, but every now and then, what you want is a no hassle number, even if it is purple. The only time a guy with that number came in, the place was dead. Snow and the late hour. He slowly sipped at his bourbon. Looked around. SIpped some more. "Where's the crowd? Where's the late night people, desperate and lonely?" I didn't know what to tell him. Sometimes the lonely, just stay at home to be alone. The guy finished his drink. In the light, the seven on his face looked to be getting more purple as he sat there. He shrugged and left to find some place else. The better place. Like there is such a place, no matter what number you got on your kisser.

The Eternal Bartender and the Cumbersome Drinkware

Bar Truth: Not everyone drank from glasses or cups, some even drank from human skulls of the vanquished.

Pat, the Eternal Bartender, replies: Yeah, that's true all the way. It don't make it right. But it is true. I was working a joint in a viking encampment, pouring mead and grog and some kind of liquor made from what seemed to be a combination of poisonous berries and old reindeer intestines. VIle stuff, but anyone who has ever had a Zima knows the taste and the mouth feel.

The joint was a nice rowdy place to serve at. But the drinkware was a pain to take care of. Now cancel the thinking that all of the folk drank from skulls. The primary receptacle was harns. Animal horns. A fella had to hold it up most of the time, and of course as the night goes on, the ability to hold on to a horn filled with mead and the thing always fell, messing up the joint awful. Now I guess for storage, you might say that I was able to stack them, but that only means you don't understand horns. Horns ain't uniform. I am sure the animal which grew them preened with pride over the uniqueness of its horns. Yeah, great, a non unique horn fits perfectly in another non-unique one, but I couldn't have that happen, no. My life would be too easy.

Hollowed out hooves were better. Hooves, generally, are not too unique. They rested on a bar top and I was able to stack them pretty easy on the bottom shelf. But the fellas didn't care for them all that much. Complained that their grog tasted a little too goaty. I thought this was a silly complaint. The vikings smelled goaty enough to my nose, who could tell if it was the booze or the boozer that wafted out eau du goat?

Washing the drinkware was easy. You gave it an angry eye and told it never to be a bad child again and then it was ready for the next customer. I miss those days. Dishwashing machines have taken so much of the joy out of the old joint. I always loved that one prissy guy coming in and eyeing the glassware and saying, "Are you sure this is clean?" A guy like that should never be allowed in a true drinking establishment. They should be working the ticket booth at a faulty ferris wheel on an uneven boardwalk.

The skulls were only used for the top shelf hooch. Skulls were designated special occasion drinking. The vikings brought their own skulls in, said all of them were of enemies they slew. That was the first part I didn't believe. I mean there was a couple scrawny guys who I didn't believe was killing and harvesting their own skulls. I saw one of them have a hard time working a butter knife and you expect me to believe he lopped off an enemy combatant's noggin?

I bet they got it from some friends who felt sorry for them. Or somewhere near the Hebrides there was a shop that sold viking tchokes. Things to bring home to the misses. T-shirts saying, "My Dad Ransacked Gaul and all I got was this shirt." A key chains with pictures of famous viking funerals on them. That kind of thing. And there on a shelf behind the register, all the skulls sat, waiting for someone to buy it and then swear it was from the head of a great British warrior chieftain. That kind of thing.

Drinking from a skull is a stupid thing. The skull must be held upside down. Now the top of the skull is not completely crack free. Pouring the booze took time. Can't have too much. Course, the drinker always insisted that more grog be put in. "It's going to come out of its eyeballs," I told them. But they got whiney. I listed the jug and filled it right up to the sockets. Any little bit of jostling and the hooch spittled out of the eye sockets.

Now I'm a bartender of some pride. I believe that I make a perfect pour. Not a drop wasted. This is what I attempt to achieve every time I uncork a bottle. To watch bad grog sloshing out through dead eye holes just upset me no end. I know the floor was dirt and no one need mop up the mess, but I felt the slosh in my inner sense of worth, And they didn't tip and they all sang lame bar songs. Boy, those vikings couldn't sing worth a damn.

I think the part that bothered me most is that each of these idiots had their own skull they stored at the bar, to be drunk from on only special occasions. The problem, they thought a long morning fart was ample reason for a special night of imbibing.

The guys tagged up their skulls with personalized runes. They said who owned which skulls. This is smart, if the drunk bastards could read the runes. I remember one ruckus with two vikings who both wanted one skull as their glassware.

They were Eric the Tooth and Eric the Greenish. That's what they called themselves. There was a big rockstar a while back named Eric the Red. He was a bloody bearded bastard who they said found Greenland. Why anyone wants to find a big shelf of ice, I just don't know. But to the vikings, finding a big land of ice makes the girls swoon and the men get aw shucks jealous. So for a time, everyone of the younger vikings named themselves after him.

Soon enough, all of the color names were full up. We had Erics of the Purple, the Indigo, the Puce. We had all of the Erics of the rainbow. There were fights by two Eric the Orange, struggling over first name rights.

It got so they had to move on from colors, and not an era too soon, I say. Eric the Tooth took his moniker because he still had one, a tooth that it. Eric the Greenish was an old school namer. He couldn't be Eric the Green, because that was taken three times over. But he did have a hue about him. He always looked like he a few too many and was ready to yawn it up. He always was tinted a tiny bit green and he embraced it.

It was a plain ordinary kind of night at the old joint, meaning there was only serious lacerations, no one lost any limbs, and if a fella lost an eye, he probably had it coming. Eric the Greenish came in and pushed a few bruisers at the bar aside, like he meant something. He said he just came back from a raiding party and brought back much for the tribe and for glory. Who talks like that? A guy who is greenish. He said he wanted top shelf grog. This of course is one the great lies of bar life. You can put the worst hooch on a high piece of wood and viola, you got top shelf. At this joint, there was only two grades of grog on tap: lousy reeking drek in a clay jug, and lousy reeking drek in wood cask.

I poured him a fine one in a large goat hoof and he tossed it right back at me. He had a lousy aim, which was not out of figure for these vikings, "I want my skull. The skull of Badderbus the Annoyed. I lopped off his head when he had the temerity to harass our raising party. When I have returned from plundering I require the test of his defeat in every draught I take."

They talked like that, all with italics and asterisks at the end to explain what he was saying. I think he was saying, give me the skull of the dude I killed. I made a souvenir cup out of his noggin and sure like the way this hooch tastes. It smells of bad mold, and it's hard to keep down, but I'm going to smile and say it tastes of victory. Did I mention that for all their plundering these vikings were pretty stingy with the purse strings?

I looked on the shelf and there was a skull i thought was his. Every bleach white skeleton head kind of looked the same. The rune on its forehead was etched lightly, it was hard to figure. WIth my back still turned, I poured in my grog and then spit in it for good measure. I mean the gonif splashed bad booze in my face.

It's the solemn motto of the bartender to spit in the glass of those who do us wrong. It's always been, and it's still the same. So be nice to every bartender no matter how soused you are.

I was handing Eric the Greenish his skull when it was wrenched from my hand and with a sudden wrist flick, all the grog in the skull flew out and hit me in the chest. This was turning into a banner day behind the stick. This was Eric the Tooth. He was a short fella. As tall as the biggest fish in most angler's fishing stories: the length of two outstretched arms. Little thing. But for all that, he sure towered over everyone with anger. Or at least he tried to. He huffed and puffed and thought all that made him taller, bigger, intimidating. It didn't, but it sure was one show. He was nearly hyperventilating to look like a man mountain. A tiny man mountain.

"Gentleman," I said, "I had a bath this season, I am sure. I don't need help on that account. But I thank you for the reminder about cleanliness. Now can you both please refrain from those gentle prompts?"

Eric the Tooth spat towards me, not at me, because like I said, they had lousy aim those Vikings. The spittle didn't even make the bar. "I care nothing for you, drink slinger, I only care that this dog is trying to drink from my skull."

"Your skull?" Greenish said, "I killed Badderbus single handed. This is my skull and I shall drink the drink of victory."

"I hear that Badderbus was drunk in his tent, and tangled his feet in the rope and broke his neck." Tooth pointed out. " And that you spent three hours cutting off his head for your own. Beavers with dulled teeth could get through the neck faster. That's a tale for another bender, for that is not the skull of Badderbus but of Tomeran the Blood. I took his head and boiled it to its gleaming whiteness myself and I thirst to press my lips on its parched bone."

"You are mad Eric the Tooth, that is my skull." He took out a dagger. That was some dagger, bigger that a small child. "I will take it or I will have a new skull to drink from."

"Fella," I said "we are pretty tight for space and we have a one skull per customer rule. So I can't have you putting new skulls in without taking your old ones away." That's me, always thinking for the betterment of my little piece of saloon.

The two Erics looked at me and laughed. I thought I had them. Laugher was always a way to get out of a bad situation. But as he laughed, Eric the Tooth withdrew his potsticker. Two huge toothpicks and their weapons, circling around each other.

The rest of the drunken vikings circled them, screaming the Nordic version of, "Fight! Fight! Fight!" The two Eircs might have wanted to stop, but they were committed. They leaped at each other and what do you know? For once in their lives, they finally got some aim. They both rammed home. Shots to the chest and the two were down.

The crowd spit in the ground. They lost out on a good fight by these two yahoos finally being precise.

Before I got from behind the stick to clean up the debris, I picked up the skull that started this whole thing. "What are you doing with my skull?" someone boomed.

I turned and there was a large slab of beard and muscle named Eric the Stewpot. "Your skull? Really. I mean these two unfortunates were fighting over it."

He laughed loud and hearty. "Of course it is my skull. My wife, Eric the Shapely, slew Gallic Joe and gave this to me as an anniversary gift. See there, that is my marking."

I looked at the rune, who knew what one was, I sure didn't. "Well Stewpot, I had no idea. I mean I never seen you asking for to drink from it. And you're here all the time."

"Why would I ask for it? I hate drinking from skulls. The grog spills and that's a sin. And besides, the edges cut out up my lips. Why would I not use a perfectly good hoof to drink from? I mean, who doesn't want that goaty aftertaste."

Who can disagree with logic like that? People tell me that no one drank from skulls. It's impossible, and I'm sure they're right. The idea of skull drinking is ridiculous. Of course everytime I mix a Grateful Dead cocktail or a Long Island Ice Tea, I have the same thoughts, that this is too ridiculous to be true.

The Eternal Bartender and the Shanghai Trap Door Slide

Bar Truth: Many bars were merely fronts to shanghai unfortunate individuals dumb enough to drink in one these and then sold and indentured as a shiphand.

Pat, the Eternal Bartender, replied: Now this is true and not true. Were there joints that a guy would come and drink a fine mikey finn and then woke up in a boat heading around the horn. A lot of the time it was something in the drink, but other times they was just hit in the head. Now the way I liked best, if I had to choose the best way to shanghai a fella was just to say "Hey fella, you got a fine face, drinks are on the house." And they gave him a full bottle of rot gut and the rummy drank the whole thing to black out. Next scene, out on sea for the rest of his life. I like that the means to the ends is about drinking, a pure method for a bad conclusion.

Now I never shanghaied a fella. I worked at a few joints that supplemented their income by doing it. But I never would help out, even when I was asked. I am a bartender. I'm not a fella to spike a drink to make a guy pass out. That's against everything that makes a bar great. What makes a bar great is the simplicity of it. A person comes in because of thirst. He gives some coins and we let him borrow a glass filled with something that will wet that parched throat. A bar makes money selling booze. That's it. A bar doesn't have a pool table or a pinball machine. A bar doesn't have trivia nights. A bar doesn't hawk pretzels or sandwiches or pickled eggs. A bar doesn't sell scratch tickets or t-shirts saying that this bar is spirited. And a bar doesn't incapacitate their customers and sell them to down and out ship's captains for much needed crew. No. A bar sells liquor. All those other things can be fine, but not for bars. Let the coffee houses have all that.

But I can get all high and mighty and be above it all, but I was working at a Portland bar back in the day that focused on bad whisky and passed out customers. I wasn't part of it. I didn't knock em on the head. I didn't slip anything funny. But I didn't do nothing to stop it. There was a bartender named Pickles who made more money selling drunks then he ever made getting them drunks. He was a fine enough little snake, and I knew to never accept his offer of drink. I was never that thirsty.

Pickles was a skinny louse. He didn't have a muscle on him. I ain't the kind that pays attention to the muscles of a guy I work with, though I would love to know there was a Charles Atlas knock off working next to me to take care of the cases of rye that get delivered and the kegs of beer that need to be changed out. Pickles, he was no good at any of that. He was also no good at picking up and putting the drunks that were knocked out and placing them in wheel barrels, to be carted off and sold. He asked me if I could give a hand. I had a little bit of strength in me, what with doing the job as long as I had. But I was waving my hand and going nah none of that. "I make drinks. I sell bad booze. I ain't working for a moving company or a slave ship. Those things are union gigs, and us bartenders are strictly non-union."

Pickles knew to not bother me after that. So it was a funny sight to witness him pulling at some unconscious guy's ankle, trying to angle him over to the back door. Not only was the poor victim unconscious and destined to a life of hard sea life for no waged, he was now full of splinter from being dragged across the bar's old wooden floor.

Now this was a dockside joint and there were tunnels underneath the establishment that led to the harbor. It took Pickles a long time to think that a trap door was the ticket. Several trap doors set right before the stools. An eyeless sloth could see the outline of the trap doors, but our clientele were not the type for awareness.

The way it was supposed to work was that Pickles would knock the guy out by hammer or hammered drink and then he would set off the trap door and roll the guy in. The guy fell eight or ten feet to the tunnels. After the first few contestants, Pickles realized that he had to do something to cushion the fall. The guys broke their arms, legs, necks. That kind of thing. The ship's captains weren't buying these guys. They were too banged up even for them. So Pickles put straw down there. After a few of them came too and simply strolled through the tunnels to freedom, Pickles assembled some cages. The guys fell from the trap door into a cell.

This was good business, not for me mind you. I really believed there was money in just liquor. Pickles thought I was crazy, but I kept the bar clean and didn't complain. That's the other thing about bartenders, we don't yap up. We are silent as a kicked in television set. The bar was making money from me being efficient with the bottles. But Pickles was raking in a profit like he could not believe. He was selling three or four unfortunates a week.

The problem with success, it breeds competition. Other bars were putting trap doors. I even got recruited to work at one. I didn't. Not that I was loyal to Pickles. I had found a spot in the corner of the bar that felt cozy. Also, I had my regulars, which is always a nice thing for a guy working a bar. Regulars in this kind of joint were a brave, immobile lot and they should be honored.

Soon the other bars were draining Pickles's custom to two shanghaied fellas a week. He had a surplus of four or five of them. He had to throw a clearance sale, with the captured guys going for bargain prices. Pickles was not well pleased. He asked a ship's captain what would get him back buying from Pickles. He made it clear that lowering the price was out of the question. The captain thought on it some, and then came up with convenience. He didn't like having to haul the guy all the way to the ship. He liked it if he could chose right by the ship.

Now the tunnels snake down the water. Pickles came up with what he thought was a cherry idea. He made a wooden chute that went from the trap door all the way to a pen by the end of the tunnel. The shanghaied fella slid one hundred, one hundred twenty feet while still passed out. He was a porcupine filled with splinters by the end of the trip. That didn't matter to Pickles, but the customers didn't buy them and picked up captured boozers from another bar with a trap door.

Pickles still was keen on the chute and lined it with tin. No splinters, but every now and again, one of the shanghaied fellas got stuck half way down. Also a problem with selling the wares.

He gave it thought and hooked up a hose that trickled down water. This made it easier for the unconscious dudes to slide down to captivity in the tunnels. They was wet. But that made them even more popular, it cleaned them a little. The buyers must have liked the improved presentation.

This new method was the way to go and Pickles was knocking out more and more of our customer base. "Some of these were decent tippers." I complained. "They were nice blokes to have around."

The other thing that happened was that a few of our regulars liked going down the shute. Conscious. They thought it was a hoot. They would go down the length and then run back here and ask to do it again. I had the idea of insisting they buy a shot of whiskey. You want a ride down our illicit chute to damnation? You gotta get a drink. Some of them didn't want another drink so they just gave me the dough and off they went down the trap door.

Our bar take exploded. Pickles wasn't too happy about that until he realized that we were finally making more money from the booze and the fee than from selling the guys in the pens.

Soon Pickles surrendered the body selling business to the competition and went about making chutes where people paid to slide down. He called them water slides and made it family friendly. I thought that was a mistake, water slides seemed like a perfect thing for a bar. It was better than dart boards at least.

Pickles became rich from creating the world's first water park. He didn't enjoy it long. He was celebrating his success in a dive near the original place, checking out the old neighborhood when the bartender spiked his drink and he was out. I heard they transported him not by water slide but on a plank of wood attached to roller skate. I guess you can say bars that shanghaied fellas helped create not only the water slide, but skateboard culture. I won't say that, because i didn't work that joint, and I ain't one to make up stories or twist things until they become one.

The Eternal Bartender and the Books Under the Counter

Bar Fact: The Guiness Book of World Records was Created to End Arguments at Bars, It compiled Facts that were always hotly contested by those teetering on the stools.

Pat, the Eternal Bartender, replies: That's not necessarily true. The Guinness Book did settle arguments that got testy from time to time. It's always a great tool to shut up two know it alls at the bar going on with what is the fastest animal on the planet. Take out the Guiness Book and be done with it. It was under the bar with the Boston's Bartender's Guide and the baseball bat. Now people just check facts and whatnot on their phones, sure that what they're finding is right, because the internet is nothing if not perfectly accurate, or at least that's what I've been told.

I still keep the large edition of the Guiness Book in the bar. Not to answer anything. I have replaced the baseball bat with the latest edition. You get handsy or belligerent in my joint, I hit you with the full force of hundreds of thousands of useless unwanted facts and figure. A wallop with that can knock out a gorilla. And, believe me, I have served my share of those.

No, the Guiness Book was created to counter another popular book that was given to most bars for free. This, as you should understand, is why it was in most bars. Do you expect publicans to spend money on a book of truth? What are we? The bedside drawer of a roadside hotel room with the Gideon's well in place? We got us sacrament, but that come by the glass.

I remember this book like it was still under my bar. Snortz Beer's Book of Things That Make You Look Smart. People monikered it The Snortz Smart Book.

This thing came out free to us publicans. It was a cheap newsprint booklet with very small type. FIlled with tons of facts and figures. Sports info. Historical facts. Superlatives, the fastest, the slowest, the fastest, the dumbest. That kind of thing. This was a bevy of stuff and people would have loved using it. The thing is. Everything in it was wrong.

Everything. Every damn piece of info was all wrong. The first president of the United States was Aaron Burr, which is crazy because he was the fourth one, wasn't he? The world's tallest man? Napoleon. The winner of the 1939 Oscar for Best Picture? Abbot and Costello Meet the Sticky Ghost. The fastest land animal? That was also Aaron Burr. It was madness, because I knew the man and he was only fleet enough to make it up to a medium jog.

Folks were fighting over what was the most popular song of the 1890s and they consulted the Snortz Smart Book and find out both were wrong, it was "Head, Shoulder, Knees and Toes." Then the shouting got into pushing and pulling and slapping and then I brought out the baseball bat and that was the end of civility.

Every time people consulted the book, there was fights and tossed beer. I actually think that was the plan by the Snortz Beer folk, they knew that no one could stand drinking their swill, but it was a decent thing to throw in someone's face. They made more money with people ordering it to toss in the puss of another bargoer than ever anyone did ordering one to drink.

Every month, I got a new copy of the Snortz Smart Book every month. This was smart because by the end of the month, the previous copy was a waterlogged, tattered mess of ripped pages. Then the new book came and it was chock-a-block full of bullshit answers as well, but different wrong answers. No issue had the same wrong answers. I figured that sooner or later, there would be an issue where all the answers would accidentally by accurate. The truth could only be a printer's error. That's the thing, the fellas consulting the book didn't care if what they got from it was right, only that the other guy was wrong. This book provided that. It also provided bruises and need for more drink.

There was a time when I was working a country estate joint. Hunting lodge attire. The folk were the rich drinkers with guns. They went out early every morning to shoot birds or foxes or peasants, I was never quite sure. They came to me around midday wanting a little something for the throat. Now one time, the group were beer makers. I liked this tpe, they knew their pints from their quarts.

One of the fellas was grousing about not getting any grouses. Said they were the fastest game bird. Another one of them called bullshit on that and then a third came up with the woodcock as the fastest. They were well into it and one of them, the guy who worked for Guiness Brewery turned to me and said, "Pat, my good man, would you have any knowledge of what the fastest game bird is?"

"The only game bird I chase, Sir Hugh, is Wild Turkey," I told him, "I catch that bird every time I try. I don't know such rot, but I do have this Snortz Smart Book. I can look it up for ya if you want."

That's what I did. And the answer they gave was the pigeon. I know, not even a squab, but a pigeon. The lords and lushes were not pleased with the answer and shouted at me and the club and at each other. There was a large deal of fracas for such gentry level fellows.

After all the shattered glass was swept away, SIr Hugh, the guy from Guinness told me his idea of making a book filled with correct information. A book proud of truth and diligence. A book to solve bar disputes with dignity.

"No offense, Sir Hugh, but where's the fun in that?"

He didn't listen to my reasonable advice and the Guiness Book quickly shouldered the Snortz Smart Book into oblivion. Too bad. Nothing like bad information for the bar goer. Like the most successful recording artist is Aaron Burr. And that you do look handsome? ANd that last shot of whisky won't bother you at all. You're fine. We need more horrible facts is what I'm thinking.

Now you might not go to the type of establishment that has enough bar brawls for you to classify them like they are animals with fancy names, but there are set designations of bar brawl. The first is the too gone argument, where you are just jawing and complaining and contradicting and all of a sudden a hand shoots out to make a point and you got playground level fisticuffs. Then there is the out of shape pugilist brawl. That's a bunch of middle age beer bellies who think they are still twenty years old and tight like a lock. Finally, we got the Hell or High Water, I Got My Bro's Back fight where everyone is full of anger and more muscle than they should have.

The Eternal Bartender and the Curse of the Theme Bar

Bar Truth: Bars based on themes can be popular and help customers find the bar and become a regular.

Pat, the Eternal Bartender, replies: Does anyone really want the success of the customers who want to go to a Trader Vic's? Who wants to go to a fake Polynesian bar, and drink fake island cocktails in fake tiki shaped glasses, that are for sale in the restaurant gift shop? You want to know what isn't a bar? It's a joint that sells tschokes in the front. At that point, it ain't a bar with souvenirs for sale. It's just a run of the mill gift shop with a liquor license. That's all it is. The purpose at that point ain't selling booze. The drinks are the loss leader so that they will come and blow thirty bucks on a Tiki cocktail t-shirt.

With that said, I have done my time at theme restaurants. I worked Bene Hauna's, surf theme joints, a Nascar themed bar, a Canadian Backwoods steakhouse where we wore name tags with fake names. There was Billy Bob, Bobby Sue, Tommy Ray, and Tammy Fay. Or at least, I think that was on a name tag. Who knows. All I remember is that one of the waiters tried to call me Mikey Joe, the name on my tag, and I slammed an empty beer keg on his head. I don't care what it says on the tag the boss puts on me, nobody calls me Mikey Joe. Ever.

Every cocktail had to be exotic and tied to the theme. So the Bull RIng, which was a bullfighting bar I worked at, had the Toreador cocktail, which was just a rum and coke for twice the price. The picador was tequila and ginger ale and be lucky if there was any change if you handed me a ten spot. If someone gave a tip over ten dollars, management required us to go and ring a big bell and shout out, "Two ears and a tail!" We wore crazy red jackets that no matador would ever get near. I looked more like a movie theater usher with visions of grandeur.

Now you're right a little bit by saying they are popular. Sure. For a bit. For a little while, going to a sock hop themed bar can be fun, but after a while do you want to stop your sad day of drinking every seventeen minutes with a mandatory, all hands dance rendition of the Twist? After a while you want to just be in the dark and drink straight whisky that's just called whisky, no fancy names. You want a stool with cracked leather, a bar that is level and true. The most popular theme bar will go out like any bullshit shooting star. They will be a hollowed out husk waiting for the next would be bar owner to come up with the next big twist, the next big theme for a bar.

Now a days, the theme seems to be bacon. Bacon in every cocktail. Bacon as a garnish instead of an olive in that martini. The mixologist idiots freeze the bacon in dry ice and crumble it into the homemade root beer flavored whisky. Pickled bacon slices where the pickled eggs used to wallow. Really, Bacon is not really a theme for a bar. It's more like an infection. Every thing inundated with bacon. Until the next bar gets baconed. And then the next bar and the next. It's like a zombie invasion, just saltier.

I can make fun of this crap forever, but the thing is the theme bar has been around for a long time. Back in Roman days, there was a big influx of Clown Themed joints. Ask me? That's what was the real cause for the Fall of Rome.

And back in the day, Pirate themed bars were the thing. Hell, there were Pirate themed bars before there were proper pirates.

Well, not the pirates you expected. I was behind the stick in Jolly Ole wherever at a Corsairs themed bar. Those were early pirates. They were getting all the headlines, so the bar investors made the joint look like a ship and we dressed up as sailors, just a little beat down. No one came. It was a dumb concept. Who wanted to go to a Corsairs bar? It was like every other nautical themed bar.

But then I had the day where the cork hit my eye. Occupational hazard, sure, but it sure was a total drag. A doctor gave me a patch. I wore it on my next shift and the customers lost their minds. "That! That! That is a pirate indeed!" the customers shouted. This was all nonsense. As far as I knew, pirates weren't known for eye patches. But they look at me, and they think I'm a pirate.

Soon enough, custom built up to see the actual pirate making cocktails. The owners thought we should go big or go home and create a real pirate look. No one knew what a pirate look was, but hey, that's what made this so easy.

They gave us dirty jackets. They fitted us with distressed tricorn hats. One guy was given a peg leg. His legs were fine. It was a fake peg leg. This got us bartenders tips, so there were no complaints. Then the owner brought in the parrot. The damn bird.

The owner went on about the pirate idea needed animal companionship. He won the damn bird on a hand of cards. They tied the damned thing to my shoulder. It pecked my neck. You try mixing up fine brandy punch with a green feathered bastard tethered to your coat. I was bleeding and I started talking with a deep drawl.

I got out of there soon after the bird. Then a few years later I started hearing about these new pirates stationed in the Caribbean. People described them as peg legged, eye patched, parrot wearing marauders. That was me, or at least that was me when I was working the theme bar.

Ha!

Turned out a few young wannabees were regulars at the that damned pirate themed joint. They loved it . They thought that was what pirates were actually like. They shipped out to Jamaica and started up as pirates, dressed like the bartenders they remembered from the bar they used to frequent.

So all the bad pirate costumes, all the people shouting out Pieces of Eight and Walk the Plank, all those people who think they look cool in an eyepatch. All the blame can be placed on the step of the theme restaurant. You might call that success. But you would be wrong. Go to a bar filled with dark wood and that pours a decent glass of brandy and be happy.

The Eternal Bartender and the Gin Soaked Library Card

Bar Truth: Many of the great writers wrote their works at the bar, or at least after they rolled out of one.

Pat, the eternal bartender, replies: That's almost too easy. Sure. Ernie Hemingway wrote stories at the bar while wearing a ridiculous beret. That's a waste of words, every beret is ridiculous. He sat there under that underdeveloped hat of his and he was so wasted, he forgot to add all the things that made stories good, like adjectives and description. More like a cheap telegram than some kind of writing. That guy. Charles Bukowski wrote when he got home after fortifying with a few toots, but he was still loaded. I could do this all day, but like I said it's too easy.

Some of the writers tried to hide their drinking from the notebook they were scritching on. Others were just the other way. They were writing proud as you please, like everyone gets green and jealous over someone making words in a notebook, and then hiding their sips from the highball glass. You ask me, it don't matter much either way, but of course no one asks me.

The literary life and bars go well together, like gin and tonic, rum and coke, drinking and paying you tab. The classics. I don't ever want to work a bar where a fella or a lady feels wrong bringing a book into the establishment. I want the book to be welcome. You ever see that Shakespeare play where the monster is greeted by the drunken fool and the foolish drunk? Don't ask me the name of the play, you should just be impressed that I can talk about a Shakespreare play.

Anyways, the monster meets these two reprobates and they get him drunk for the first time. And they introduce the fella to the fine art of drinking. But they call the bottle a book and taking a swig is to them, "kissing the book." That's how it is. A good bar is drinking a good book. You get the crazy of the characters, the ups and downs, the fall from grace, the struggle to reach the top shelf. Nothing but a good story told in glasses. Instead of chapters, we got fingers. Instead of volumes,we got fifths. Instead of a book burning, we got a last call for alcohol. Guess which one I think is better?

I worked a joint during one of the prohibition times where we hid the booze in the books. I can't remember which prohibition time it was; there are always ugly winds that blow dry seasons from time to time. It might have been America in the 1920s, but it could have been Germany back in Luthor times. Who knows? The thing was, the prisses and the pinch faces were taking away my livelihood.

The blind pig or the speakeasy I was working wasn't anything of the sort. It was a library. It was this old building filled with books to the rafters left abandoned. I guess in times of no liquor, those in charge have no time for books. I guess they don't care for shelves holding treasures, no matter what treasures.

At first, we hollowed out big old books and fit the bottles in them. We then scattered the books around the place. The customers came to me, the eternal librarian, with a book request form. They put in a request for Pilgrim's Progress, that means I get the books and pour them a snoot of bourbon. Cocktails had several book requests. Pride and Prejudice and the Compleat Angler was scotch and soda. You want a gin and tonic? Then you're the type to want to check out The Compleat Angler and Carry On Jeeves.

I was pretty clear about the book requests, if they got it wrong, they got themselves a poor cocktail. If they asked for Jeckyll and Hyde with a side of American Tragedy, then you would be given a cocktail of Zambucca and Tequila. And as the head librarian and bottle washer, I would insist you pay for it and drink it, so that you learn your lesson. Literature is not anything to mess with lightly.

Now at first we just cut the books to fit the bottles, but people got upset for a time. They didn't like that you couldn't read the books. That the stories were ruined. I mean, what's a decent bar without a good story to share it with.

So we found a printer to design the books with the holes for the bottles already in it. All the text was around the enclosure. So you get the book and the booze to kiss, if you were in a smooching mood.

A few folk came in and said they just wanted a scotch and soda and didn't want to bother with codes or Dewey decimal systems. Just a goddamn drink. I would tell them to repeal the dry laws and they can ask for anything the way they want. Until then, pick a goddamn book or shut up. To be fair, those were fun days. When drinking and reading were war buddies together, hunkered shoulder to shoulder in the trenches.

Course the bar came back. The bar always comes back. That's a given. But people don't read in bars as much as they should. We have TV and Juke Boxes and cell phones with Candy Crush on em. I look at a person come in with a book and ask for a glass of something, I want to kiss them. Like the book would want to. Books are friendly, smoochy types, and who's to stop them?

The Eternal Bartender and You Don't Have to Go Home But You Can't Stay Here.

Bar Truth: Bars close when town ordinance says so, there is no real time for a bar to truly be closed.

Pat, the Eternal Bartender, replies: Got to tell you. You are wrong there. Sure. There are laws for each state of when the bars have to shut. But there is a definite optimal closing time for a joint. That's at 2:35 in the morning. Not a minute before it. Not a minute after it. 2:35 in the morning.

That's when all bar going turns sour. 2:36 and that pretty girl you're talking to, turns ugly. That's when everyone's politics is wrong. I mean more wrong than usual. That's when you look at that ugly sunken mug in the mirror, the one that was looking fine and happy just a minute before and you wonder, "Why are you hanging in there with me? Don't you have somewhere better to be?"

Wars have started after the optimum closing time. Divorces. Marriages. One bris happened at a joint after that true and honest closing time. I didn't work that joint but I believe it all. You tell me that it happened at 3 in the morning, I will tell you, sure, I believe it. I try to get everyone out at one thirty in the morning. Some tight bastard or another will get all high and mighty at me and wonder why I'm pushing them out, and I say to them, "Buddy, I'm trying to save you a world of hurt and flesh wounds. The end of times are coming, and you want to be home before that happens. The end of times happens every night. There's a daily armageddon and you want to be home before the antichrist shows up and starts showing you pictures of his kids."

You might blame the time of night and the amount of booze, but I know that ain't so. There is a real reason for that. 2:36 was the time on the clock at the bar at the Center of the Universe right when the big bang happened.

Ah, big bang. I hate that name. There was no bang. There was no air, how could there be a bang. That's just mass marketing for you. The same advertising firm that pushed Cinco de Mayo as a day to quaff agave drinks and told you that Zima was something to drink, as the one that said the beginning of all time was a bang. Big bang, pah! It was more of a rush to the bathroom then a bang. It was a long line for relief is what it was.

Now back before time began, we had the same problems at a bar as we do now. Nothing is much different. You got to get asses in seats. Which is how the Bar Promotion was born. Before the beginning of the Universe and there was already: Ladies Night, Wet T-Shirt Contests and Disco Dance Offs. Hell, there wasn't any light to glimmer off the mirror ball, but still there was Disco Dance Offs. Weird, unpleasant evenings, which just proves things haven't changed much.

Now, this one bad promotional idea came from the owner of the Center of All Things, the joint I was working behind the stick, not there were any concepts of directions back then, but work with me. He said Saturday Night was going to be a hell of a promotion, Penny till You Pee. The idea was you paid ten bucks to get in and once inside every beer and cocktail was just a penny until someone used the bathroom. At that point, the prices went back to normal. This was a bad idea, because it was going to be so popular. You don't want your bar promotions to go gangbusters or big bang busters, you want them to be pretty alright at most.

All of the theoretical concepts and astronomical uncertainties heard about it and came through the door. Their pockets were so full with pennies, they were all walking in at angles. They all came with empty livers and iron bladders. The place was packed. Everyone wanted a penny drink. These were not my finest cocktails, but what would you expect from drinks for a cent. Also, no one thought to tip, I mean they were figuring that they should tip fifteen percent of a penny, which was just another mathematical concept, nothing to take home and pay the rent with.

It was all hands on deck and we were still not making drinks fast enough. Making matters worse, the owner realized that there was a shortage of bartenders so had the door guys and bouncers come and help us out. They were slow and confused, and worse yet, that left the doors unguarded and every fella and dame from the before time sidled in. Everything before the Big Bang was there in that one bar, and they all had pennies to splurge with.

No one could figure out where one drunk patron ended and the next drunk patron began. It was like they were all fused and it was just one drunk acting crazy, waiving pennies in the air.

We were pouring bad drinks. I mean the drinks weren't bad, they were fine concepts of drinks, like gin and tonic, whiskey and soda, negroni. Those concepts were fine. But we were pouring all these slipshod, fast and thoughtless. Can you blame us? We had everyone shouting for the next drink, the next drink, hey over here, and all that insistent nonsense. The calls and the screams were so loud and pleading, I wasn't even hearing them. And to speed up, I was screwing up the proportions of the drinks

That's important to point out. Getting the proportion to mix drinks isn't just to make a decent cocktail, but the right amount of each element keeps the universe in balance. You put too much gin in a Long Island Iced Tea, not only will it taste bad, I mean worse than it usually does, it will shimmer the walls of existence. You laugh, but I know of a couple worlds that blinked out of the fabric of the real without a how de do, because some overworked bartender made a martini with too much vermouth. Dry martinis aren't just delicious, they protect the fabric of the heavens with every well proportioned sip.

That goes to say we weren't pouring right,and ripples of uncertainty began to appear all around us. Not that we noticed. Fella was busy making drinks and taking pennies for the effort. It sure felt like it was a metaphor for something or other. Now in the period before the Big Band, everything was just a metaphor. Especially the time when they were in a bar doing the pee dance.

Oh the pee dance. The move of hips. With everyone so close to each it was impossible to figure out who needed to pee and who didn't. One mathematical equation went for the head and he was stared down by a couple gas giants. Gas giants have big pockets for pennies and didn't want to stop. This went on for a while with folks giving up and trying to pee and the gaseous masses blocking the bathrooms.

I figure this was against the rules, but rules are not anything worth worrying about when you're drinking for cheap in a spatial singularity. This was going on longer than anyone, especially the owner figured possible. He was losing a fortune. It was now 2:35 in the morning.

But folks needed to pee and they were drunk at this point and that's when politeness and gentility go out the window. And that's what all the drunken patrons did. They rushed the windows. Pushed down the walls ran to find some place private to pee.

The problem was, there was no private places. Everything was nothing. So they just kept running and running and running. Moving ever outward. The entire universe was going out looking for a private place to pee and that happened at 2:36 in the morning.

The universe is still racing out, which is crazy, you think they would have a found a good quiet place to relieve itself by now. But I'm just a poor publican, what do I know.

I know that 2:36 is the time that drinking should stop. And even now, to this day, someone passes a penny at a me for a drink, I will throw them out. Faster than the beginning of time.

The Eternal Bartender and the Fruity Frozen Frothy Furor

Bar Truth: A male bar patron must identify what is a girly drink in the current bar culture and avoid it, less he will be in a world of trouble.

Pat, the Eternal Bartender, responds: It takes a powerful, muscle bound bloke to go into a biker bar and order a champagne cocktail. He's got to be a strong, decisive fighter to do that, and if he's going to really do it, he should drink it with his pinky out all nice and genteel. That's the way it should be done. But it don't happen like that..

I can see it in some of the customers' eyes as they are drinking a whisky sour or a gin and tonic. Their overly hoppy IPAs that is so astringent it can be used as embalming fluid in a pinch. These poor bastards are drinking their manly drinks in big gulps, but their eyes are saying they want to have a toasted almond or a midori sour. Don't let the name fool you, it's not a sour drink, its liquid candy and off limits to the men. These men dream of daiquiris and bottles of the finest Zima.

The umbrellas aren't to blame, but I think they contribute to the problem. I mean if you put a paper umbrella on it, you know that that is not a manly drink. That's a parasol warning sign. That's to say danger ahead. People working at a reactor put up those incomplete triangles that say be careful round here, bucko, there is radioactivity around here. People working a bar use paper umbrellas the same way, you are drinking condemned material with a fast half life and a high sugar count. You see an umbrella and there is a possible manly fight about a girly drink in the near future.

I have a theory of how it all began. I was an eyewitness to some of it, but you know, there ain't no research grant out there to try to figure out why certain drinks are girly drinks. You know what, I don't like calling any drink girly. Some drinks girls like. Some drinks bearded galoofs prefer. But don't blame the drink. The drink is tasty, be it sour or sweet or strong. A cocktail has no gender. It's an unisex entity. It can go into any restroom. So it's not right for me calling this a manly drink or a girly one.

Back in old England time, the big drink were sweet things. Punch. That's a kind of drink that was a big thing back there and it was a fine thing to make. It wasn't made by the glass, I only made it in a large batch and just ladeled it into the glass. That's class and efficiency. They had names like Pimm's, Smoking Bishop. Fish House Punch, Planter's Punch, Cups and whatnot. They were sweet and tasty and if you had to give them a name, friend, they would be girly. They were sweet and they were pretty looking. Put an umbrella on it, and you would be happy to drink one of them at Ladies Night at the local Ground Round.

With popular drinks that bartenders can make ahead of time, you know this traveled. Had to. Went across to America. New York and Baltimore and those towns drank this up. And then for some reason, it moved west. Some drinks have wanderlust. They can't stay still and look at the same stools and the same grubby hands pawing their glassware. They want to see the sights. Go out and see if there is a better joint to be the featured libation in. Checking the drinks circuit. Shaking a leg. They want to make their name on chalkboards across the land. You know the old saying, the glass is always chiller on the shelf. You don't know that expression? Then you are as refined as I thought you was.

I was working one of the mining towns, in a big bar filled with dirty sons of bitches. They all tried to pay with the gold they found. I was having none of it. I am old fashioned, I pour only for coins. Now, I'm pouring four credit card and who knows, maybe I will be pouring for bitcoin or something I ain't even thought of, but that seems to me like so much fool's gold. Like a lot of the nuggets of shiney nonsense they slammed down on the bar and shouted to me, drinks on the house. I would cry, not on your life. Get a shower and find yourself some real money. They would be ornery, but if they wanted to drink where I was pouring, they got to singing the tune that I picked. I mean who's to know what that nugget really is. It could be painted up tinfoil wrapped around some chewing gum for all I knew.

It was a tough place and the fights were breaking out all over. They also drank fast. Real fast. They were ready for the next snootful even before they was done ordering the first. I was rushing around that bar like I was on roller skates. There was one moment that I thought that strapping on wheels wasn't a bad idea. They were slamming their coins down shouting for whisky or some cocktail. I was getting wiped out. I was happy for the custom and the volume, but these miners were lousy tippers. Any kind of prospector always is a lousy one for showing gratitude to their barkeep, be they gold miner or fourth guy in at a biotech start-up, they are always tight on the purse strings. So I was forced to do a lot of this volume for just the barest of remuneration. I was getting hosed for all the moving and pouring I was doing.

But I have me a memory and I remembered those wonderful punches that you can mix in a large batch The ingredients weren't tough to get and I made up some Cups and some Smoking Bishop and a sweet brandy based number I came up with on my own that I was fond of calling the Felonious Alderman.

The rabble wasn't too keen on trying this at first. I considered giving them a free shot of it, on the house. But then I remembered the bartender's edict about giving the good stuff away. So instead I offered them a punch, and if they said no, I would punch them. Beat hell out of them until they said, yeah sure, a punch sounds like a good idea. And if I hit them to try the damned thing, I charged them double. I said, the beating is cost prohibitive on the bartender and you best pay extra.

They drank it. And they paid me and I was happy. A couple of those stone tongued imbibers had the damned gaul to tell me that it was a little sweet. A little too much. Not to their liking. For that they got another wallop from me. And after that, these dumb miners realized the great joy and benefit that was a punch. I mean the drink punch.

You might not understand, but part of the job is to guide the drinking public into what is expected at that bar. At this bar, I wanted them to drink their punch and be happy about it.

And that was my part of it. I can only guess how the rest of it came to be. People learned that certain drinks was tied to violence. I hit them to like it, and that was how they thought of it. I mean, it is called punch for God's sake. You figure you drink it you get punched.

People got worried about drinking something that was tied to getting punched so they would have the bartender mark which was a sweet punch with something on the glass. That's how the paper umbrella got into the picture. You see the paper umbrella on a glass, that there is a sweet punch and you will be punched sweetly.

And then the ladies working the mining camps tried the punch and liked it. Of course these were tough dames and you didn't punch them. You didn't even look at them sideways if you didn't say please and thank you. They were not to be trifled with and if they liked a sweet drink called a punch, then damn if that's what the ladies drank.

And because of these tough broad working ladies, the punch and all sweet drinks got the bad rap that it is girly. That's a laugh because they were not girly. They were not even girls. They were women who knew how to belch and fight and spit and drink daintily.

And if a guy wants to have a white russian with extra russian in there, I say, that's a tough drink. That's what a real tough guy will drink. And to think the stigma came from English punch that was drunk by roughly painted women, I say, that's a thing of pride. A thing of beauty. That's worth sitting down and ordering a double for.

The Eternal Bartender and the Terrible Generosity

Bar Truth: There is nothing better in the drinking life than someone coming in and ordering drinks for the house.

Pat, the Eternal Bartender, slams his hand down and shouts: Now that's a damn dirty lie and I have cut people for saying less. And I truly mean cut. I remember seeing a sign in a dirty biker bar that read "Anyone selling drugs in the bathroom will be cut." This caused a lot of discussion about what it meant by cut. Did they mean they were cut from the genteel list of attending the bar? Did it mean that someone went outside and slashed the tires of the guy's bike? Did it mean the guy was to be forced to get a trim from the town's worst barber? Or did it mean that there was going to be a knife used?

To be fair, I don't know what cut meant in that case. And I don't care. I never worked that bar, so let those who do frequent that joint worry about the true definition of words. For me, I can tell you that when I say that anyone who wants to order a round for the house on my watch will be cut with a knife. Now I might not be the one doing it, but there will be cutting, and there will be a knife.

Do you get it that I slightly disagree with this ridiculous bar truth. Bar truths. You are giving me things you might have heard at two in the morning, five drinks past reason, and you are calling them bar truths. There are no bar truths really, I wasn't going to tell you, I just like talking, and I figured that your bar truth concepts weren't a bad thing to get me started in my yapping.

But I put my foot down when you say that rounds for the house are good and wonderful. You're acting like the day when someone bought you and everyone there a round was the best day of your inebriated life. Like it was Drunk Christmas.

Just think of the whole idea of drinks on the house. Think about it logically. Some idiot rushes in, excited because, he getting married, or he's getting divorced, he won a big court case, he got out of jail early, he is finally in love, he gave up being a cheapskate for lent, he recently discovered the word racecar is a palindrome and he wants everyone to celebrate such an amazing thing. Drinks on the house. Drinks for everyone. Makes everyone happy. Everyone but me.

I'm the guy who has to make all these drinks all at once. And everyone wants something special for the special occasion. There will be no orders of Bud drafts for this Drinks for the House fiasco. They will order drinks with five liquors, with each floating above the other, like they were the strata of all the cities of Troy. They will order champagne. They will call their buddies who are at the bar down the street to come here quick like and come in the back and swear they were at the bar the whole time and can he have the top shelf single malt. I mean the guy said drinks on the house.

Some guy comes into a mostly empty joint and joyously orders drinks for everyone. Before he has finished his sentence, the bar population has tripled. It's an amazing thing, people should do studies on this amazing example of Saloon Teleportation. People appear out of the mist when free drinks are offered. That's the scientific paper that I want to see. Something useful for once.

Let's tackle this with as much logic as we can stomach. How will I know if the guy can pay for it? I insist on seeing a lot of bills or a credit card and then I am going to call and make sure that it can hold this amount of liquor. Then I am going to take the guy by his ears, pull him close to my angry red face and ask if he really wants to do something so costly and for what? For strangers to like him? And the answer is usually a pathetic "Yes, Drinks for the house?" Yeah, they usually turn that last one into a question. And this is all before I pull a single drink. Most of the time I take money in advance and say I will return the unused sum at the end of this ordeal.

Then I take a pad to tally the cost. I tell all of the grinning idiots that when they heard drinks for the house, what they really heard was one free drink that has to be a draft beer or a one liquor cocktail. The top shelf is off limits and if you don't like it, then you can pay for your own drinks you cheapskate sons of bitches. That shuts them up mostly and they hangdog ask for a better than they usually get beer.

Then there are the guys who drink their beer toot sweet and hide the glass under their stool and say they would like their one free drink and no they didn't get one. And then I tell them nuts to you and then start fighting and arguing and acting like that drink is their right. And then to explain to them that drinks on the house is not plural for them. The drinks is everyone having one drink, not this one bozo getting enough for the long winter's night.

And then it's over and the guy who done it in the first place is disappointed. No matter how great it was to shout "Drinks for the house" he is still just a guy by himself, at a bar. Nothing going to change that. A Rockefeller or a Carnegie is a just enough man to fill one bar stool. Showing you got money to burn ain't going to change that truth, be it a bar truth or otherwise.

I could stop there. That is like the end of a drunken tirade, but I don't think you fully comprehend the danger and folly of ordering for the house. Nonsense like that has caused the ruin of civilizations. Hell, the big Wall Street collapse happened because of some full of himself bond trader ordering drinks on the house. That was the day before the big collapse. We all know Black Tuesday. It all really happened on Mashed Up Monday, at a blind pig I was working down the financial district. This was still prohibition time.

With that said, this speakeasy I was at was decent enough. They had a real bar for me to work behind, which was a nice place for me to be. I don't feel like myself when I am bartending a converted butcher shop, or front room to some bachelor apartment. Give me a bar with bottles behind and a mirror to make it look bright and opulent, that's where I should be.

This wasn't that exactly, but for 1929 Wall Street, it was close enough that I didn't weep myself to sleep. All of the traders and bankers came in after the stock exchange closed. Some came before starting, to fortify themselves. Others came all day and didn't leave. These were the financial geniuses. If you don't believe me they was geniuses, ask them, they'd tell you. That's all that said, they were geniuses and they were practically printing money. They weren't concerned that they were leveraged past tipping and the London Market just tanked. No, not them. They knew the market was as solid as their marriages and their mistresses. These were confident idiots and their words were as oily and slick as the gunk they slicked down their hair with.

But you got to understand I knew something bad was going to happen. People were leaving booze on the bottom of the glass. That is the sign of a distracted drinker and a distracted drinker is not just a poor customer but a harbinger of doom. If I read the papers I had known that the market was going to belly up, but I'm a bartender and the only I do with a newspaper is use it to clean the mirrors behind the bar.

Finally, sometime late on Monday a group came in all hangdog. They knew it was coming and they knew didn't have the money to pay off their debts if the bubble popped. They sat there listening to the piano player and they just stared off into middle space.

The door blew open and in strutted this high end investor. This is the king of the exchange. This schmuck with a smile. He looked around, "There is nothing to be down about. We got the best market in the world and it's solid like a Carnegie library. If there was would I be here having a drink? Would I be here paying for everyone's drinks? No. I would only do if I knew the market was humming along. So here goes. Barkeep. Drinks for the house. Everyone drinks on my dime."

And faster than you can say margin call, more bankers and investors swarmed into my small establishment. The place rocked. Men were shouting for drinks, the kind that wouldn't make them blind. We went from 75 people to five hundred or more. There was a crush. People were pushing toward the bar.

Now the bar was not built into the floor. This was a speakeasy, it didn't have to follow government guidelines on construction. It was just a slab of wood put before the shelves of booze. They pushed onto the bar and moved back quickly and with force. I popped out of their like a cork from a bubbly bottle and landed on top of the crowd like I was an early example of crowd surfing.

The bar pushed into the shelves and went through the wall. It was ticky tacky walls and of course that was a support wall. The whole building started buckling. People fled out of there, though there were still some of them standing there for their drinks. The cops and fire department came and evacuated the building which shuffled down into rubble.

It was the news of the investors, that there was a crash on Wall Street. That was how it was talking about. So when trading started the next day, people were even more shaken than usual and sold all of their stocks shorts and the banks tried to get the investors to settle up on their margins because there was a crash on Wall Street. And that helped make the real crash happen. Things got better the next few days and then on Tuesday it really crashed.

Now people tell me that it was going to happen anyway, but let's be fair. The stock market crash happened because some banker dunce ordered drinks for the house.

So just don't do it. Drinks for the house can topple an economy, and is a free glass of well booze worth that?

The Eternal Bartender and the Fire of Hell and Other Exaggerations

Bar Truth: The right name for a bar ca n aid in its success.

Pat, the Eternal Bartender, replies: This can't be any more true. I mean you go to a bar named Frank's and that is all it is. It's a bar named Frank. It might last a few years, maybe even a few moves, to smaller locations. But it ain't going to make it. But you name the place the Matador, or the Pelican Club and you are printing money my friend. What makes a good name is the harder part. Pete's is not a good name for a bar. Mel's is. Why is that? It's a universal constant, like calculus. You don't have to understand it, you just gotta know it is true. Partner's, bad name. Drinking Buddies, good name. The Back Room, bad. Gold Coast, good. 3Gs? Must I say? You see? And if you do, then you are better than me. A good name is hard to find but if you do trip over one and call it yours, you will do well in this world my young friend.

Take the Hellfire Club. That famous drinking club back in the London of Olden Times. The Londen of wigs and laced sleeves. that was so notorious and blasphemous. Now let me just stop here for a second and say that blasphemy in bar terms is a different thing than in the greater, more holy world. To me, something that is blasphemous is mixing a good gin with half bottle of Diet Coke. That is something to be excommunicated for. String em up, I say.

But going to a bar and drinking and eating and chasing girls with low necklines ain't blasphemous, even if they said the president of the club was the devil. I met the Devil once, he was at a bar I was working in Chicago during the 1968 Democratic Convention, and what was the Devil with his horns and pitchfork and his brimstone cologne, what was that Devil drinking? Hamm's beer. And he paid with pennies and nickels. So let's not take the Devil as this sophisticated man of wealth and taste as doctrine.

The Hellfire Club, the first and only real one, was around for a few years and met most of the time at the Greyhound, where I practiced my trade. It is the most famous club of revelers outside of Peter the Great. And let me tell you something, they were a dull and boring lot. They were better than sleeping pills.

People might say they danced with demons, drank with abandon and caroused like Kennedys. But that's just PR for you. They drank weak tea with the occasional splash of Spanish wine. If they spilled a little they would say, "Darn it." Or "Gosh I mean God Damn." They were never good at being bad. They played backgammon until closing. They would blush when a woman walked by on the street and cried to high heaven when they got themselves a paper cut.

They were so dull I thought it was hell. They tipped great, with the caveat that if someone asked I had to say that these Hellfire folk were mad and crazy and full of mad wanton desire. They were abominations, that's what I was to say. And I did. With my eyes rolling like they were dice in a loaded craps game. But I said it and I guess the sarcasm in my responses were lost with the ages. They were bad boys and it was all because of the name. They were the Hellfire Club and that's how we remember them. If we were truthful to their true selves their name would be the League of Foppish Nerd Boys and no one could ever look at them with awe.

That's what a good name can do for a joint. Though, I would not want to work at a place called the Hellfire Club nowadays. I have a problem pouring drinks at a joint with chains and whips. I did do that once, but I ain't talking about that saloon right now. Ask me a bar truth about bars and dungeons and I might bring out that amusing anecdote. Or maybe I won't. It might not be time for that story. Ever.

The Eternal Bartender and the Technology of the Bar Stool

Bar Truth: The bar stool was one of the ways that kept people at bars longer, thus increasing the bar business.

Pat, the Eternal Bartender, replies: I guess that you can call the bar stool a technological advance in the world of bar going. Before the bar stool, people stood and lingered. They just bellied up the bar and some of them really did belly up to the bar. Their bellies, back in Roman Senator joints, were enough to hold them up without their feet touching the ground. They wedged their big old veritas wine bellies into the edge of the bar top. Wedging your belly up against the bar was a way to ensure that you didn't fall down drunk.

Now the really swanky bars in Rome had benches for the rich, but they were never used. No man about town wanted to have his lower than the next one, so it might as well have been a bar for galley hands and freed slaves with no one sitting down. Everyone tried to look taller than the next guy. Let me tell you, there were a lot of guys in togas standing on tippy toes, jutting their necks out like giraffes.

They stood until they couldn't, those drunk ass Roman Senators. They were sloppy drunks, as most people dressed in bed sheets tend to be. They drank some nasty strong fortified wine, the wine of the gods they called it. Wine of the Gods. What they quaffed down was the ancient world equivalent of Boone's Farm. But that's politicians, they hold their liquor almost as good as they hold up the common good.

This is just me saying that this poshy joint full of senators was just wall to wall guys standing and pushing into each other. We had large pillows in the side room where they could lie luxuriantly and be fed grapes. Well, they tried to have people feed them grapes. Mostly, the people standing around ignored them, possibly farted in their direction. I don't know that for certain, but that pillow room stank something awful. I'm thinking farts. Or it was just the fact that the senators and the hangers on didn't know what to do with water and soap. They would bathe in communal baths all the time, but truth, they just weren't good at it. The whole cleanliness concept was a tough one back in Roman numeral times.

They did know how to drink standing up and not collapse on the ground. They knew that if they fell down drunk, the trampling was all they had to look forward to. If they fell down and flattened like pita, then all I had to look forward to was a thorough and mostly pointless of the now bloodstained floor. Cleaning up bloodstains, always the toughest and no doubt, truest aspect of the bartending arts.

Now this was the bar that Nero, or one of those guys, was playing his bass fiddle while there was a fire going around. Course, I'm not talking about the fire, not too interested because our joint wasn't bothered by it, with us being up wind from the flames. Despite the gossip of the day, Nero wasn't on a hill watching it blaze, no he was at my joint, drinking too much and not paying his tab. But he was the head guy, and the head guy can get away with not paying. They shouldn't, but they do. I know more coups and revolutions started because there were unpaid bar tabs than I care to bring up.

But like I said, this ain't about the fire. I didn't have to cash in on insurance, so it really is nothing to worry about. No, I bring up Nero because he helped create the whole concept of the bar stool. Him and his fiddle playing. If you can call it that. It was playing like that they made bartenders invent the jukebox later on down the line. There is nothing worse than live music by regulars who think they have talent.

He helped create the bar stool because he came in all the time to play his instrument and he loved the attention. To him, Nero loved nothing more than a standing room audience. He thought people standing all around was a sign that he should play longer and louder. "Oh you want more do you?" And then he imitated a flayed cat with his bow and fiddle. He had a talent. At making the worst sound ever. Not everyone can be that ear bleedingly bad. I guess that's what made a fella a Caesar, poor ability presented as art.

All the senators and high falutin Romans there couldn't do anything, stand or be trampled and so they went to Pliny the Elderberry for help. He was this scientist and writer that was always soused on elderberry wine. Sometimes folks were too exhausted from talking and drinking to use his full name so they just said Pliny the Elder. He had a twin brother who preferred wines from young grapes, so they called him Pliny the Younger.

Now Pliny the Younger was too drunk too do much thinking so they went to Pliny the Elderberry with the dilemma. They spoke to him, "Pliny, old beam, we want to continue drinking at this joint but the great and blessed Caesar insists on killing our ears with his bluegrass scratchings. He likes it best if his audience is standing, he will play more when we do. But if we sit, we will be trampled and that's not a good look for this season. So how can we sit and show dissinterest and not get a big fat sandal in the face?"

And that's when Pliny the Elderberry created the bar stool. That wasn't his first idea. He first invented the barcalounger. But it took up too much room and there could only be six or seven in the joint. He then paired back and built a bench in front of the bar. This was better, it got a lot of folks sitting down, while not laying on the floor. But the problem with a bench was that they were Senators and men of means and they didn't want to share a seat with anyone else, even if it was with another senator. Especially because it was another senator.

So back to the drawing board for Pliny the Elderberry. He was in cups one day, in a slight bit of desperation, when he saw some working fellas shipping knock off busts of Venus to sell in the adult shops in the sticks or in Gaul. The Gaul always liked them naughty Roman busts shipped in brown paper and sold under the counter. Actually, they were shipped in wooden crates. And the crates gave Pliny a lightbulb. Well, he didn't invent the lightbulb, but that was his brother and that is a story for another bar. But Pliny the Elder came up with the solution.

He upended the crates and put a little padding on the top. There was no reason for the padding, but the clientele were a soft lot so needed a soft place to land. He cut out some of the middle planks of the crate so the legs had somewhere to go and the remaining plank on the bottom was like a foot rest. Hell, it was the first foot rest. He painted it green, because that was the stain he had on hand. And that was it. The first bar stool. All he had to do was push a ton of them around the bar and with their shape, a lot could be stationed there. And the folk flocked to them. It was the place everyone wanted to be.

When Nero came in, all the guys at the bar instinctively learned the move I have seen from that time on. They created and enacted the oblivious drink focus. That's where the guy on the bar stool stared at his glass of booze intently, like it owed him money. So intently, that he couldn't notice anyone else around. Like say, a crazed Emperor with a knock off Stradivarius.

Nero was annoyed. No one was watching him play. They just sat at the bar communing with the wine glass. Maybe that's why he burned the town down, he had to up his performance game. He wanted everyone's attention while he played. So he had to burn down the whole town to do it, but hey, if you want your music to be watched at, you got to go big I suppose. I guess that's why even now all the rock bands bring out the pyrotechnics. Got to shoot off some fireworks to have people listen to the noise they call music.

Well I guess Nero inadvertently invented two big innovations: the bar stool, and the over top Eighties hair metal concert. Damn that Nero.

The Eternal Bartender and the Last Drink Before the Knife

Bar Truth: Before the introduction of surgical anesthetic alcohol was a means to help patients, with some hospitals in France housing bars for their patients.

Pat, the Eternal Bartender, replies: Yeah. That was mostly the case. More to the truth was that there was a hip flask of some serious grappa or grain alcohol that was ready for a guy going to be cut up. Losing your arm to amputation? Well, have yourself a snort of the good stuff. Or the bad stuff. As long as that stuff was heavy alcohol and that it was going to deaden you enough to not feel the bone saw.

Who are we kidding? You are awake and having your arm sawed off? All the bourbon in Kentucky is not going to stop you from screaming to high heaven.

But there was a time when surgical advances were moving faster than the advances in deadening pain. They were doing amazing plastic surgery but no way to make you not feel every cut. You know when they say, the first cut is the worst? Well they were lying. The deepest, longest, last cut is always the worst.

There were some hospitals in Paris that set up dispensaries for the numbing needs of the patients back in the early 19th century. I worked one for a bit. And let me tell you, that was a great bar to work at. The people coming in were very focused on the drinks and what I can do for them. A lot of the time at bars, the bartender and the drinks he makes are secondary or tertiary. Hell, sometimes the drinks are not even on the list of things to consider when at the bar. It is not the important part. Meeting friends, getting out of the house, trying to make it with the preferred person just before last call. Reading the paper and checking box scores.

Not at the dispensary bar. I was the main attraction. I was the reason people could even consider going forward in life. They needed that toot or three to make it through the bone saw and the four muscled palookas holding them down. Most of the time, I expected my clientele to come to me on their own power. To walk right up and say, "Pat, give me something to deaden it all." Here, no one came to me on their power. Folks were rolled in on chairs or gurneys. They sidled up the bar as much as their wheeled apparatus allowed. The focused intent on me and what I made was gratifying.

A bartender can't often say that pouring the next cocktail is a matter of life and death. In this gig, it was the case. Now most of the surgeries of the time didn't make a big deal of the doling of the booze. They just thimble fed them table wine or poured a toot of whisky from the bottle directly into the mouth.

But that kind of attitude was degrading. This Paris dispensary bar believed the customer, or patient if you want to speak the patter, demanded respect. So with that in mind, I was in pressed whites. My apron was a thing of starched, blinding beauty. My mustache was waxed and twisted into tips so sharp, I could use it to remove wine corks in an emergency. I was what the poor customers in the gurneys were looking for. I was made for the part.

I asked, "What do you want on a nice day like this?" I usually got a laugh and something like, "Give me a stiff one." And who would be mad enough to blame them. They weren't going under the knife so much as under the saw. And for that, I will make you a fine drink.

I discovered the perfect drinks for each operation. Whisky for leg amputation. Lesions, grappa. Removal of scar tissue, that was a modern cutting edge surgery at the time, so the only thing was a cutting edge cocktail, and that's when I invented the corpse reviver. The original kind with calvados and cognac. It's the hair of the dog. It revives people to a better state. That's what I told them, and I always gave a fancy explanation, my patter knows no peer. But the truth of the matter is that I made a strong drink that would numb them up and I just thought corpse reviver was a funny name.

The big problem is that while I came up with these great strong cocktails to help them get through the surgery, all these French patients wanted was wine. A glass of wine. A splash of burgundy s'il vous plaît. And then they would get upset if the wine was not up to snuff. We got people waiting to go and cut off their leg and there they were complaining that the vintage was not right. It is a poor vintage. Like your leg, was something I always wanted to say. But that was poor timing so I kept quiet and found another bottle of wine for their liking.

And when they went into surgery, I still had a nice business going from the onlookers who suddenly needed liquid strength when the screaming and scraping started. There was always a full auditorium when the surgery began thinking that it will be a fun show. But halfway through there was a sudden rushing toward me and my humble bar as they demanded grappa or gin or something strong. Something that made them deaf and blind.

I always have that. That is the staple to my trade. The deadening glass. No two versions are alike. It's the results that matter. I make a fine killer of senses. I don't use it much for surgeries, the hospital bar racket died out when ether came in. Not that I believe in ether or anesthetic that you need to inhale or inject into your system. That's no way to have a good time. But I use those same skills still. I pour a lot of the deadening glass the day after elections.

About the Book

Pat is the Eternal Bartender. He has worked at juke joints, mead halls, and floating barges filled with beer. As long as there have been public places to drink, Pat has been there with his white shirt and surly attitude.

He can tell you stories about how bars used to be. And he will. All you need to do is tell him some bar lore and he can steer you straight. He can tell you how he helped create the Sandwich. He might divulge what the bar at the big bang was like. He can confess about the time he got napkin drawings from Picasso to pay the bar tab.

There is a long history of bar life and Pat knows it all, because he was there. So sidle up to the bar and ask him some questions and Pat will answer. Just remember to be polite. And tip, dammit. You have to remember to tip.

About the Writer

David is finally getting some of his ald manuscripts out. Why was this not published when he wrote in 2017? No one knows. He kind of just forgot about it. It was not that he wasn't writing and publishing. He has put out over 130 ebook titles. That's a lot of nothing, sister. They have been short novels, themed short story collections (like this one), How To Be A Good Writer books, pop culture studies, and weird crap that no one is sure should have been put out. This book and most of the others were not written for anyone other than David. He writes for no audience but himself. It can create some wild and odd books. It can also allow him to forget to publish a book for seven years. But don't worry none about that, the book is done and you have read it (or skimmed it at least) and now you can put his name in the internet machine and ind other weird ass books he created.

www.ingramcontent.com/pod-product-compliance
Lightning Source LLC
Chambersburg PA
CBHW022105150726

47990CB00003B/1255